WALT DISNEY'S

LITTLE

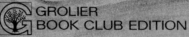

GROLIER
BOOK CLUB EDITION

First American Edition

Copyright © 1978 by The Walt Disney Company.

All rights reserved under International and Pan-American Copyright Conventions.
Published in the United States by Random House, Inc., New York,
and simultaneously in Canada by Random House of Canada Limited, Toronto.
Originally published in Denmark as LILLE HIAWATHA OG DEN STORE FISK by Gutenberghus Bladene, Copenhagen.
Copyright © 1977 by Walt Disney Productions.

ISBN: 0-394-83848-3   ISBN: 0-394-93848-8 (lib. bdg.)

Manufactured in the United States of America

GHIJK   6 7 8 9

HIAWATHA

Little Hiawatha was a very small
Indian brave.

One night he saw something that
made his eyes grow big.

The older braves were dancing
around the campfire.
They were chanting a strange song.

Little Hiawatha ran into his father's teepee.

There sat his father, Big Chief, and his sister, Sunflower.

"Father!" cried Little Hiawatha.
"Why are the braves dancing tonight?"

"They are dancing a fish dance,"
said Big Chief.

"Tomorrow there will be a fishing
contest," he went on. "The brave who
catches the biggest fish will get to wear
my war bonnet and be chief for a day."

Little Hiawatha
smiled proudly.
"I will catch
the biggest fish,"
he said. "I will
win the contest."

"You are too small to catch a big
fish," said Sunflower. "I will help you."

Little Hiawatha scowled.
"Sisters are a lot of trouble,"
he said. "I don't need your help."
Sunflower just smiled.
Maybe she would help and
maybe not!

Little Hiawatha stamped out of his father's teepee.

"Sunflower thinks I am too little to do something big," he said. "I will show her!"

That night Little Hiawatha dreamed
that he caught a huge fish.

In his dream he got to wear the chief's
war bonnet for one whole day.

Early the next morning
Little Hiawatha went to the lake,
where he kept his canoe.

He was carrying his fishing pole.

Little Hiawatha paddled his canoe
out onto the lake.

"When I am chief for a day," he
thought, "I will make Sunflower work."

As he paddled along, many fish
leaped out of the water.
But they were all too small.

Little Hiawatha was looking for
a really HUGE fish.

Suddenly he heard a loud SPLASH.
There it was—the biggest fish
he had ever seen!

Little Hiawatha picked up his pole.
Now it looked very small.
The fishing pole was not strong
enough for such a huge fish.

Then he had an idea.

He grabbed his rope and made a loop at one end.

He tossed it over the big fish.

SWOOSH! The fish slipped through.

So Little Hiawatha tried again.
This time he swung his rope high.
This time he flung his rope right.

And this time he remembered to pull
tight.

ZIPPP! He caught the fish by the tail.

The fish tried to swim away.
Little Hiawatha hung on to the rope.
He went for a fast, jerky ride.

But at last the fish was too tired
to swim any more.

Little Hiawatha tied
the rope to his canoe
and paddled to the shore.

He tied the other end of the rope
to a tree.

Then he ran home to get a net.

Sunflower was going to the lake
to wash a basket of clothes.
"Hi, Brother!" she said happily.
But Little Hiawatha did not stop.
He was running too fast.

Sunflower walked on toward the lake.
"Little Hiawatha is acting very silly,"
she said. "Brothers are a lot of trouble."

Down at the lake there was another
kind of trouble.

The fish was trying to get loose.

Sunflower dumped the clothes on a rock
and set her basket on the shore.

Just then the fish made one last leap.
It landed in Sunflower's basket.
Sunflower was surprised.

"Why, this fish is tied up
beside my brother's canoe,"
she said. "It must be his.
I will take it to him."

She covered the fish
with a blanket so it
could not jump out
of the basket.

As Sunflower
was walking home,
Little Hiawatha
ran by with
his net.

"Come and see how I am helping you," she called.

"Don't bother me," cried Little Hiawatha. "I am busy."

Sunflower was angry.
She looked at the fish.
"I will teach that brother
of mine a lesson," she said.

She took the basket to Big Chief.
"Here is a fish for the contest,"
she said.

When Little Hiawatha reached the lake,
he picked up the rope.

"The fish got away," he said sadly.

Out he went to fish again.
But at the end of the day...

he had only one small fish to take home.

As he came into camp, Little Hiawatha
heard the news.

The winner of the fishing contest was
SUNFLOWER!

Sunflower got to wear the war bonnet.

"Look at the big fish your sister caught," said Big Chief.

"That's nothing," said Little Hiawatha. "I caught one much bigger but it got away."

The next morning Sunflower became
chief for the day.

"As Chief, I will put you to work,"
she told her brother. "Wash the clothes."

Little Hiawatha trudged off with
the clothes basket.

"This is terrible," he thought.

"My sister gets to tell me what to do."

But when he came back, Sunflower
told him the whole story.
"That huge fish is the one you
caught," she said.

She told Big
Chief, too.

"I wanted to teach my brother
a lesson," said Sunflower.

She put the war bonnet on Little Hiawatha's
head.

"Now that you are the chief today," she said,
"I hope you will be nice to me."

Little Hiawatha just smiled.

Maybe he would be nice and maybe not!